Sporty Bunny Tales

Grosset & Dunlap
An Imprint of Penguin Group (USA) LLC

GROSSET & DUNLAP
Published by the Penguin Group
Penguin Group (USA) LLC, 375 Hudson Street, New York, New York 10014, USA

USA | Canada | UK | Ireland | Australia | New Zealand | India | South Africa | China

penguin.com
A Penguin Random House Company

ISBN 978-0-448-48036-7   10 9 8 7 6 5 4 3 2 1

It was garden-party day at Grandma's house. Ruby
and Louise set up the tables.
"Baseball!" said Max.
"You can play with Roger, Max," said Ruby.

"Let's play catch!" said Roger.

Roger showed Max how to catch the baseball in his mitt.

"Catch!" said Max.

Ruby and Louise brought out sandwiches.

Suddenly . . . *Swoosh!* The baseball came zooming by. It almost hit the sandwiches!

"Max!" said Ruby. "Can you play away from the garden-party table, please?"

Max and Roger went to the other end of the garden.
"Throw and catch!" said Max.
"Here it comes!" said Roger. "Fly ball in the air!"

Ruby and Louise brought out punch and glasses
for the party.

Suddenly . . . Roger's fly ball landed inches from the punch bowl!

Max went under the table to get it.
"Thanks, Max! But can you play farther away?"
said Ruby. "How about behind the fence?"

Ruby and Louise brought out the cake and put it on the table. The guests began arriving.

Roger threw a curveball. It bounced off Max's glove. "Oh no!" said Roger. "The baseball is heading straight for the party!"

Everybody in the garden looked up. They saw the ball in the air.

"Oh no!" said Grandma.

But Ruby made a miracle catch!

"You saved the day!" said Grandma.
"Fastball!" said Max.

Ruby Works Out

"Hello, Ruby and Louise," said Mrs. Huffington. "Now, to get your Bunny Scout fitness badges, you'll need to touch your toes ten times, run in place for ten minutes, and jump for the sky ten times!"

Bounce, bounce, bounce!
Max bounced his basketball on the court.

Oops! The basketball got caught in a tree. Ruby
and Louise jumped up high to get to it.
It took ten jumps to get the ball out of the tree.

"Great jumps!" said Ruby. "We've done the first step for our Bunny Scout fitness badges!"

Bounce, bounce, bounce!
Roger showed Max how to dribble the basketball.

Ruby and Louise jogged in place.
Bounce, bounce, bounce!
The basketball went right past them.

Ruby and Louise chased after it. It took them a while to run it down.

"We did the second step for our Bunny Scout fitness badges!" said Ruby.

Roger showed Max how to make a basket.

Ruby and Louise were touching their toes when . . .
Bounce, bounce, bounce!
Along came the basketball again.

It went over Louise, and then it bounced into the trash can!

"Good basket!" said Roger.
He got the ball out of the trash can.

"Max," said Ruby, "can you and Roger play basketball back over there so that we can finish our exercises and get our fitness badges?"

But Mrs. Huffington came running.
"I've been watching you, Ruby and Louise!" she said.
"Your exercise in basketball rescue and avoidance gets
you a fitness badge each!"

Ruby and Louise cheered. They were so excited to get their fitness badges.

"We didn't even need to follow each exercise,"
Louise said.

"We just needed Max and Roger!" Ruby said.

Ruby's
Home Run

Ruby and her friends were going to play softball near the playground.

"I'm going to get a home run, Max," said Ruby. "Just you watch!"

Ruby went up to the plate. She crouched down and waited for Roger to pitch to her.

Just then, Max's windup plane came wobbling by over Ruby's head. Ruby swung her bat, but she missed the ball.

"Strike one!" said the umpire.

Ruby asked for a time-out.

"Max," said Ruby, "I'd like to hit a home run, but I won't be able to with your airplane flying by. Can you play with your dump truck instead?"

Ruby went back to the plate. Roger was waiting for her.

Ruby swung at the next pitch.
Zoom went Max's airplane again, right under
Ruby's feet.

Ruby took another time-out.
"I have only one strike left, Max," said Ruby. "Can you please not play with your airplane?"

This time, Max sent his rocket over Ruby's head.

Ruby swung her bat, trying to avoid Max's toy. She hit the ball with her eyes closed.

Ruby ran around first base, second base, and third base to home trying to catch Max's rocket.

Ruby gave the rocket back to Max.
"Next time, Max," said Ruby, "can you keep your rocket and airplane home and play with some other toys?"

"Home run!" said the umpire
"Really?" asked Ruby.
"You hit the ball over the fence!" said Louise.
"And you ran around all the bases!"

"Wow!" said Ruby. "I really did it!"
"My turn!" said Max.